ELMER AGAIN

David McKee

Lothrop, Lee & Shepard Books
New York

Elmer, the patchwork elephant, was bored. It was two days before another Elmer's Day — the day when elephants cover themselves with bright patterns — and all the elephants were quietly thinking about how they would decorate themselves. But Elmer didn't have to think. He was always colored gray for the Elmer's Day parade.

"It's too quiet around here," said Elmer. "I'm going for a walk."

So Elmer set off down the path. "We need a joke to liven things up," he thought, but no good jokes came to mind. Just then he came to a pool. He looked down at his reflection.

"Hello, Elmer," he said to himself in the water. "You've just given me a good idea. Thank you."

When he returned, the others were still quietly thinking. Elmer walked over to his friend Harold and whispered in his ear. Harold smiled and winked, but said nothing. Then Elmer settled down for a rest. He had a long night ahead of him.

When night fell, Elmer waited until the others were asleep. Then, taking care not to wake them, he set to work.

Before sunrise, he had finished. He tiptoed off to another part of the forest to sleep for what was left of the night.

In the morning, the first elephant to wake looked at his neighbor and said, "Good morning, Elmer."

One after another, the elephants woke. "Good morning, Elmer," each one said to his neighbor. "GOOD morning, Elmer." "Good MORNING, Elmer." "GOOD MORNING, Elmer." "Good Morning, ELMER."

During the night, Elmer had painted all the elephants to look like him. Now there were Elmers everywhere, and nobody knew which was the real one.

"Are you Elmer?" the elephants began to ask one another.

"I don't know," the elephants answered. "I might be today, but I'm sure I wasn't yesterday."

Then one of the elephants called out, "This is another Elmer trick. Come on! Let's splash across the river and wash off the colors. Then we'll see who the real Elmer is."

The elephants raced to the river and splashed to the other side.

But when they got there, they were *all* gray.

"Where's Elmer?" they asked.

"Here, of course," said a gray elephant. "Don't you recognize me?"

"But you're the same color as us," gasped the others.

"So I am," said Elmer. "Wonderful! I always wanted to be like you."

"This is awful," said the elephants. "Elmer can't be like the rest of us. Things won't be the same without a patchwork Elmer."

"Well, there's nothing I can do about it," said Elmer, "unless . . ."

"WHAT?" cried the others.

"The colors that washed off are still floating on the water," said Elmer. "If I run back through them, I may return to normal."

"Try it!" shouted the others. "Try anything to get your colors back."

"Yahoo!" called Elmer, and he raced across the river and vanished into the trees on the other side.

In a moment he reappeared, once again in his bright patchwork colors.

"Hurrah!" cheered the elephants from across the river. "It worked. We've got our Elmer again."

They began to chant, "Elmer! Elmer! Elmer!"

Suddenly another elephant came out of the trees. "Did you call?" he asked. He was soaking wet, as if he had just run across the river.

The other elephants just stood and stared. For a minute, they didn't know what to think.

"*This* Elmer is Harold!" said Elmer, and he and Harold began to laugh.

The herd of elephants burst out laughing then. "We should have known our Elmer's colors would not wash off," they said.

Then they all jumped into the river to celebrate *two* Elmers, and the whole jungle shook with laughter at the best Elmer joke yet.